CULTIVATING POSITIVE PEER GROUPS AND FRIENDSHIPS

ADAM FURGANG AND KATHY FURGANG

rosen publishing's
rosen
central

NEW YORK

Published in 2013 by The Rosen Publishing Group, Inc.
29 East 21st Street, New York, NY 10010

Library of Congress Cataloging-in-Publication Data

Furgang, Adam.
Cultivating positive peer groups and friendships/Adam Furgang, Kathy Furgang.
—1st ed.
    p. cm.—(The middle school survival handbook)
Includes bibliographical references and index.
ISBN 978-1-4488-8311-0 (library binding)—
ISBN 978-1-4488-8317-2 (pbk.)—
ISBN 978-1-4488-8318-9 (6-pack)
1. Age groups. 2. Friendship. I. Furgang, Kathy. II. Title.
HM721.F87 2013
302.34—dc23

                                                                2012017872

Manufactured in the United States of America

CPSIA Compliance Information: Batch #W13YA: For further information, contact Rosen Publishing, New York, New York, at 1-800-237-9932.

CONTENTS

INTRODUCTION

So, you've made it through elementary school. Congratulations. You can look back at your first day of kindergarten and say to yourself, "Boy, I've really come a long way." But now you're in middle school and ready for a whole new set of challenges. You know it will be different, but you're not really sure exactly how elementary school and middle school will differ. That uncertainty makes you nervous, and, as a result, the whole situation is less exciting and gratifying than it should be.

Well, first you need to know some of the most basic differences between elementary school and middle school. Not to freak you out, but most likely your middle school will be considerably larger than your elementary school. The students in the elementary school you came from will likely be dumped together with students from two or three other elementary schools in your area, and you'll have to deal with more, more, more. Confusing mazes of hallways will greet you at the crack of dawn. And don't forget the rows of lockers that will make you wonder which one is yours and how on earth you will get it open.

The kind, sing-song voices of your caring, encouraging, and nurturing elementary school teachers have been replaced with harsh ringing bells that tell you its time to get up from your desk, get moving, and don't be late for the next class. Instead of the arts and crafts of your elementary school, its time for an agenda notebook filled with dates for tests, reports, and assignments.

You will meet all kinds of new people, too. Let's call these new people you meet your peers. These are the classmates and kids you see every day in your homeroom, in study hall, at the lunch table, in your gym class, and in every after-school sport and activity in which you take part. There may be hundreds of kids in your school. They are all your peers. It takes good relationship-building skills to turn a peer into a full-fledged and true friend. In middle school, you need to walk the tight-rope between peer and friend and not fall off. Not all of your peer relationships will be friendships, but they are both equally important for getting along in middle school.

For instance, getting used to your new science lab partner and the kids on that new soccer team are important if you want to get along with peers. At the same time, you have to make sure you still spend time with your old pals, too. Middle school gives plenty of opportunities for things to get mixed up and confused between peers and friends—not to mention old friends and new friends—but with a little guidance, you'll be ruling the school in no time.

After all, middle school is still just school. And you've got plenty of experience going to school already. Getting used to middle school won't take forever. It will take some people longer than others, but remember that everyone is going through a difficult transition. You may see kids that you think have their acts together, but don't be fooled. Every single student is adjusting to the same challenges. The trick is to survive it with as few scrapes and as much grace as possible.

CHAPTER ONE

PUTTING THE "SOCIAL" BACK IN "SOCIAL NETWORKING"

Y ou've had friendships since you were a toddler. But things are a bit different now. Your mom doesn't set up play dates for you and help you settle every little argument over a toy block or sippie cup. For quite a while now you've been making your own friends, arranging your own get-togethers, and working out your own problems. Sure, you still need a ride to some of your friends' houses, but you are becoming much more independent in your friendships and relationships. So, what do you need to know about the next phase?

Change Is the Only Constant

You may not know it, but your friendships may be about to change, in some cases dramatically. You are being exposed to so many new things at middle school and so many new people, that your

Middle school is a great chance to meet new friends while still being surrounded by old friends from elementary school.

tastes and your friends' tastes may be changing or even growing apart. But don't worry; it's not the end of the world. Growth and change can be good things, and you should look at this as a positive and necessary process.

Your best friend from kindergarten may still be really into the games you used to play when you were younger. He's only into video games, but you are getting interested in girls. He likes playing soccer, but you want to be on the football team. She is into clothes and makeup, but you want to play sports. She wants to go camping, but you want to go to the mall. The world is bigger for you now, so there are more interests to choose from. You may be bored playing the same old games, but your friend may feel that you are not being as fun as you used to be. These may just be growing pains for your relationship, and they do not need to signal the end of your days as friends.

From Stranger to Friend

Just as you are meeting more people at school, so, too, are your old friends. You may be sitting next to a kid in math class who is really funny and treats you well. He comes from another elementary school, so this is the first time you are meeting up with him. He then introduces you to a bunch of his friends, and your circle of friends suddenly widens a bit. This exposure to new people and viewpoints, to new energy and possibilities, feels like a breath of fresh air.

But think of the other scenario. You sit next to a kid in math class who is rude and annoying and makes your days miserable. He thinks you hair looks funny and he doesn't like your clothes, and he thinks it's his business to tell you so. He's not exactly

A lab partnership may provide an opportunity to meet a new friend or start a new peer relationship in your school.

bullying you, but you get a rotten feeling whenever you are with him. Instead of meeting new friends through him, you feel that running into his friends in the cafeteria makes your queasy feeling grow even more sour. You feel pessimistic and hemmed in by negativity, judgment, and rejection.

If you are experiencing something like the second scenario, you need to think of a way to get that creepy guy out of your mind and concentrate on the things that make you happy. There are plenty of other friends and peers around, so keep looking for the ones that make you feel good instead of bad. The best-kept secret about awkward peer relationships is to just go with the flow. The more relaxed you are about the situation, the better. Friendships

SIBLINGS: FOR BETTER AND FOR WORSE

What's worse than having an argument with your brother or sister at home? How about having one at school, in front of all your teachers, friends, and peers? When siblings go to the same school, they may run into each other at after-school activities. If you get along with your sibling, this can be a great thing. But if you are constantly at each other's throats, make sure that you don't bring your home problems to school with you. It could get you into trouble with teachers who are trying to keep order and maintain harmony in a club or sports group. If you think being on the chess team with your older brother will cause him to tease you or cause trouble, try some other activity in which you can shine on your own without having to meet up or compete with your sibling.

Remember too, though, that older siblings can sometimes be helpful when you feel that you can't go to your parents with a problem. Siblings have been through the situation you're currently experiencing more recently than your parents and may know some of the kids or teachers with whom you are having a problem. If you feel like you can trust your sibling and his or her judgment and advice, try to open up and seek help from him or her.

happen naturally, and not everyone is a good match. Just relax and try not to give the guy anything to latch on to and make you miserable about. If he senses he's getting to you, he will torment you even more. Don't give him that power. If he senses his needling of you is not achieving the results he'd hoped for, he'll move on.

One of the trickiest parts of starting out in middle school is knowing which people to let into your world. While you may be seeing less of your older friends, you are also constantly trying to judge new peers and deciding whether they would make a good friend or not. It is not an easy decision, and it will require some trial and error. But the effort is worth it, and it is a necessary part of finding your way in a new environment such as middle school. Give everyone a try until you have found the deal-breaker reason that someone would not make a good friend. Some of these red flags might be sharply differing interests or the other person's association with fighting, bullying, drinking, drugs, or other activities that you know you need to steer clear of.

While you are trying to adjust to the new middle school workload, new teachers, new hallways, and new schedule, you will also be making choices about whom you surround yourself with. This is an important issue, so leave no stone unturned in your search for the best friendship group possible.

Group Work

Many middle school teachers like to make students work together—group projects, group reports, group study sessions. It can be fun for some, but others can dread experiences like this. A person who works well alone can find himself or herself in a position of having to lead a group of students or, worse yet, follow along as part of a group. This can be difficult for those who work faster than the average student, as well as those who work slower than the average student, not to mention those who like to control and perfect every detail of an assignment.

Study groups and group projects are a way to meet new students, but they may also be a challenge in terms of focusing on academics rather than socializing.

Getting through a group project can be a challenge, but it is important to realize that many people feel the same as you do. Stay calm, keep your cool, and just focus on the work. It will be done in no time. Try to make the assignments as fair and evenly distributed as possible so that one person is not left doing the work for everyone. If you find that your group is just not getting along and can't work out their problems, let the teacher know. Try not to let a bad group experience ruin your grade, your under-standing of the material, or your interest in the subject matter.

Great Minds Think Alike

Think about all of the possible student groups that you can asso-ciate yourself with in middle school. There are likely more clubs, team sports, and other after-school activities to be part of than there were in elementary school. There's every kind of sport you can think of. There are bands, orchestras, drama clubs, singing clubs, scouting groups, outdoor clubs, arts and photography clubs, church groups, and countless other academic clubs from chess to computers to science to math.

One thing many tweens do before joining new groups is to think about how the group will positively or negatively affect the "image" they are trying to build for themselves. Don't fall into that trap. Do what you like, do what makes you happy, and don't worry about what other people think of the group or its members.

Finding people with the same interests as you can help you make the most of your middle school experiences.

You may join a group to be with your friends, or you may join because you happen to know a lot about chess and love playing it. Be yourself, and you'll find that you are surrounded by like-minded people who may become new friends. The point is, when you stay true to yourself and hang around other people who have the same interests, you will become happier and more involved in what you are doing. You will spend less time worrying about what other people think and whether you are doing something "uncool" or that annoys or angers others.

Social Networking

One thing that sets life in middle school apart from elementary school is social networking on the Internet. As you enter the tween years, more and more students from school will join social networks and get involved in chatting and socializing online. There are plenty of useful and valuable things about being online. It can be a good way to keep in touch with old friends from elementary school that you do not get to see very much anymore during the school day. It can also be a way to get to know new friends better. Be sure to get your parents' permission to have a Facebook or Twitter account and to add new friends or followers.

If you are old enough and are given parental permission, it can be fun to keep up with friends online. You can get to know friends on Facebook by checking out what they "like," how they update their status, and whom else they are friends with. Updating your own status and photos can in turn give new friends and acquaintances a better sense of who you are.

As a general warning, however, don't take everything you see online as the absolute truth. The online world is not the

Social networking is a way to connect with people, but it provides its own challenges in terms of getting to know what someone is really like.

real world. Someone with seven hundred friends on Facebook is guaranteed not to be close with all of them. He or she may not even be particularly sociable in person. That person may still need a good friend in real life to handle the transition to middle school just like you do. And just because someone indicates on Facebook that he or she "likes" a rock band or singer that you detest, it doesn't mean that the person is someone you can't get along with in real life. A person's online profile can say some things about the person, but it does not provide anything like the complete picture of what that person is truly all about. Knowing what he or she likes does not tell you what his or her personality is like. It doesn't let you know if the person is shy or outgoing, if the person is kind or mean, or if the person can be a true friend, face-to-face.

The Virtual You

Remember that when you are online, you need to be the same kind of person you are in school or in person. There is something that feels different from face-to-face conversation when writing your ideas and feelings on a keyboard and pressing "send." When you are online, there is a lot of human connection that is lost. People can't tell as easily when you are joking. Some people won't be able to judge your tone or meaning as well as other people can. And some people just have a lot more courage to be rude or insulting online than they do in real life.

In the online world, there is less adult supervision and protection. It is easier to insult or hurt someone's feelings. Some people take advantage of that feeling of power and freedom. It may be too obvious to say, but keep this in mind: those people are not your real friends, and they are peers to stay away from.

There have been many cases where tweens and teens have been bullied online, sometimes to the point of suicide. This can happen because of young people's inexperience with online communication. Instead of risking a confrontation in the school, where a teacher or other adult could intervene, some people think they can get away with picking a fight with someone online. But the arguing does not always go as unnoticed as people might think. Many other people can read the comments and conversations that take place on a public wall on Facebook or on a Twitter feed. Making fun of someone or falsely accusing a person of something is a form of bullying. The evidence is out there for everyone to see, including the friends and family members of the person being bullied. Whatever you do online, remember that others can see your comments. Bullies are noticed online. They destroy other people's online experience, and they are hurtful. They could be hurtful to a good friend of yours, or they could be hurtful to you.

There is no need to be friends with people who do not treat you well, either online or face-to-face. Unfriend these people. Block them. Report them. If they are bothering a friend of yours, make sure your friend blocks and reports them also. Most times this course of action will take care of the problem. If a person then begins to bother you or your friend in school because he or she can no longer harass you online, you have a better chance of reporting the person and getting adults who can do something about it involved. Bring the argument to the attention of someone in a position of authority. Don't handle it by yourself, and don't get involved in a war of words online.

Think of that the next time you want to get involved in a public conversation on a friend's wall. Make your comments reflect the kind of person you want to be known as. If you want to be an encouraging, helpful friend, communicate that way online. People often feel more comfortable saying unkind things online because they are not doing it in person. But always remember that what you say on Facebook, Twitter, and other social networking sites is a reflection of who you are.

CHAPTER TWO

AFTER-SCHOOL LIFE

You've done the best you can with learning to open your locker and remembering all of the new teachers' names. You've figured out how to work effectively with your new lab partner in science class, and you've become Facebook friends with fourteen new students from your school. Things are beginning to settle down. So how can you continue to develop and refine a positive, healthy, and lively social life at school and cultivate enriching new friendship and acquaintanceship groups that you can be proud of? Easy: remember that your school life goes on even after the ringing of the final period bell.

Extracurricular Activities

After-school activities, also known as extracurricular activities, can be just plain fun. They are designed to enrich and broaden students' learning experiences, and this includes being in social situations with other kids. Believe it or not, being social takes practice and finesse. No one is born a social butterfly. It can take

Getting involved in sports teams is a good way to find new friends and develop new relationships.

years of being in school and social groups with peers before you can truly navigate a social scene skillfully. The first step, however, is getting involved.

Instead of going straight home after school, think about getting involved with a club or sports group that you enjoy. You might love to swim or play baseball, soccer, football, or golf. You might like to act, sing, or dance. You might like to draw or take photographs. You might like to create code for your own computer programs or build robots and remote controlled airplanes. You are limited only by the activities offered by your school and your own schedule. As long as you can handle the workload and the playload, get involved in as much as you'd like.

THE NEW KID IN TOWN

It's hard enough making the transition to middle school from elementary school, but when you are also the new kid in town and in school, the challenges can be compounded. If someone new to your town starts going to your school, make a special effort to get to know the new student and make him or her feel welcome. Introduce the new classmate to people you know. Think about the difficulty everyone has with adjusting to middle school. Then add to that the necessity of starting out knowing no one at all. Put yourself in the shoes of the new person. That new person may even be you one day! Treat him or her as you would hope to be treated. You may even end up acquiring a new best friend.

Remember that some activities involve auditions or tryouts. You may be competing with friends when you try to get involved in extracurricular activities. For example, you and a friend may go out for soccer. Your friend may make it, but you may not. You may get a part in the school play, but your friend may not be selected. Remember that extracurricular activities are ways to meet new people, but they may not turn out to be the opportunity you hoped for to hang out with your long-term best friend.

Don't be afraid to try something new without the comforting presence of your best friend. Keep doing what you enjoy, and you will meet new friends, while still hanging on to your old ones. Your world is getting bigger in middle school, and there is room for more people in it. You can be sure that you won't be close friends with all of the kids that are in your after-school groups, but be open to the possibility of making a few new buddies, and it may just happen.

Party Time!

Middle school is a time when the previously all-boy and all-girl parties get mixed up and mashed together. Some kids may not be interested in hanging out with the opposite sex, but others will be excited by the prospect. Parties with dancing and other coed activities can be fun when you are with old friends or new acquaintances. As you get older, these parties will be more

Middle school is a time when friends of the opposite sex may begin to attend parties together, mingle, and date.

common. If you have friends who are not yet into parties where boys and girls mingle—or if you're not into them yourself—don't worry; there will be more time in the future for such parties.

The reason many kids like these parties is because they are becoming more interested in dating. Crushes are common in middle school, and you may even be asked by friends to find out whom someone is interested in dating. This is all normal and part of the middle school territory. Remember, though, that boys and girls can be friends with each other without dating, and not everyone is ready or even allowed to be dating yet. There will be plenty of time for dating in the future. If students are dating already, make sure that they are not left out of social groups after a breakup. Middle school breakups are common, so no one should be excluded from friendship groups because of the people they dated in the past.

Cliques

When the school year gets under way and the after-school activities are in full swing, students sometimes notice cliques forming.

While cliques may appear to provide friendships to the members of the group, they tend to exclude other students. It may even be an isolating experience for some clique members.

A clique is a small group of people with shared interests who like to spend time together. Sounds, nice, right? Well, a clique is also a group that does not like to let others in. It can be difficult to overcome cliques. Some schools have more cliques than others, and it can be uncomfortable to be around people who don't want you to join their circle of friends.

In a way, after-school activities can contribute to the formation of cliques. Kids on the football team spend a lot of time together. Cheerleaders do, too. They have many of the same interests and friends, but this is no reason to exclude other people. Cliques can be noticed in classroom situations, in the cafeteria, in gym class—anywhere that students gather.

So what do you do if you want to join an after-school activity that is known for its exclusive cliques? Simply think about the group you will be joining instead of the students you will be with. Does your interest in the group outweigh your discomfort with the clique? Some groups of students may seem more intimidating than they actually are. They may band together simply because they have been friends for so long or they grew up in the same neighborhood. Try to find out about the history of their friendship.

You may find that some of the clique members may actually welcome a new person and the fresh energy and perspective he or she provides. A clique often has one or two leaders that the others follow. The people follow the leader and his or her wishes because they lack anything else to be inspired by. If a new person with similar interests came into the group, the dynamic could change, and that could be good for the clique. Remember that the identity of the group is not the same as the identity of its individual members. Give people a chance and see how they act. If they make choices that you would agree with, they might make a good friend.

Chasing Popularity

On the flipside, if you can't penetrate the clique, don't keep trying. A group that won't let anyone in is not one that is worth trying to join. Every school has a clique that may be known as the "popular" kids. Entrance into this charmed circle of popularity is highly coveted. The members of the group tend to have an attitude that indicates that they think they are better than their peers. This superior attitude can affect both those who belong to and are excluded from the clique.

People who believe that the "popular" kids are better than everyone else are likely "followers" who want to be part of the group. After all, who doesn't want to be the best? But after taking a close look at the group and its activities, attitudes, and behavior, you will probably realize that the clique's members are concerned with the wrong things and that they are not better than anyone else. Nonetheless, the popular cliques take great pleasure from excluding others from the group. They feel this gives them enormous social power. Being exclusive is one of the key traits that define them. So they go on making others feel bad that they do not belong in the inner circle.

Being in a popular clique can often be confining and restrictive for its members. They have to do whatever the group tells them to do, wear what the others are wearing, and date and be friends with people the group approves for them. They are not growing as much as they should at this age, and they are not becoming

It takes strong individuals to avoid cliques and gangs and to take their own social paths to find healthy, supportive, and sustaining friendships.

strong individuals. They are more dependent on others to tell them what to think and do. And they shut out others who might open their minds to new ideas, interests, and viewpoints. So if you can't get into the popular clique, you might want to breathe a sigh of relief instead of feeling bad about it. Cliques are a major source of peer pressure and negativity in young people's lives. And who needs that kind of pressure?

Gangs

Speaking of social groups that tell you exactly what to think and do, gangs are an extreme version of the clique. A gang is a group that may be involved in illegal activities such as drug use, theft, and violent crimes. Gangs are most prevalent in cities or high crime areas, though they are increasingly common in suburban and even some rural areas.

The gang will often pressure people to join it by claiming to offer protection from harm. Gang members may even threaten a person's family or friends if the person does not join the gang. There may be difficult, dangerous, illegal, violent, or humiliating hazing activities that are part of the gang initiation process.

If you are approached to join a gang, make sure you tell an adult who can help you and advise you on how to proceed and stay safe. You should also consider notifying the police or having a parent, social worker, guidance counselor, or school principal do so.

MYTHS and Facts

MYTH

If you are a nice person, you will have a lot of friends.

Fact

A nice person may very well have a lot of friends, but it is not guaranteed. The number of friends you have does not matter as much as the quality of your friendships.

MYTH

Being in the popular group would make life in middle school easier.

Fact

True friends should be able to make your middle school life easier, but being in the popular group actually has nothing to do with that. Being in the popular group will not make your life easier unless the friends in your group are really true friends.

MYTH

It's not cool to be smart.

Fact

When people pay so much attention to sports and much less to academics, and when "jocks" are much more likely to be popular than "geeks," it might seem that nobody respects or admires a smart person. But when you grow up, you'll see that the cliques that existed in school no longer exist. There is no cool or uncool. Adults can be a lot more mature than middle schoolers, and intelligence and knowledge are almost always rewarded.

CHAPTER THREE

BEING A GOOD FRIEND

Now that you've joined a few clubs and made a few friends in middle school, how do you build and strengthen these new relationships? Being a good friend is one of the most important skills one can learn, as is being the kind of person that others can trust and admire. It may seem obvious, but people often need to be reminded about how to be a good friend. You have to treat others as you would like to be treated yourself. Be supportive, forgiving, and thoughtful to your friends. In turn, they'll do the same for you.

Support Your Friends

Transitioning to middle school is a challenge, as you already know. But think beyond your own difficulties and consider the challenges your friends are experiencing. Are they encountering the same problems you are? Chances are they have their own issues that are cropping up. Maybe your best friend doesn't like his new teachers. Maybe he keeps getting in trouble by forgetting

A good friend is a good listener who is sympathetic to the problems of others. If you are a good friend to others, you can expect the same respect and support in return.

his homework. Maybe he can't for the life of him remember his locker combination.

There are thousands of things that can stress out a person in a new school, so stop and pay attention to how your friends are adjusting. Take time to talk to them and compare experiences. When your friend hears how you are doing and you share stories, experiences, and impressions, you may be able to make each other feel more at ease with the new and unfamiliar situation. Knowing that you are both going through it together helps ease the anxiety.

Support your friends in other ways, too. Try not to feel threatened by the fact that your friend has decided to join groups or clubs that you don't want to be a part of. It doesn't necessarily mean that she is growing apart from you. If your best friend from elementary school wants to be a cheerleader and become part of the popular group, remember to think of her feelings. Don't put her down because you don't support the same groups or interests. Encourage her abilities and make her feel good about going after what she wants. Be there for her if she is disappointed, too. If she doesn't make the cheerleading squad or if she is turned away by the popular clique, don't be the kind of friend who says "I told you so." Being supportive means that you understand and empathize with your friend; it's not about being proven right.

You may even feel your friend slipping away when he or she gets involved with new friends at school. These new friends may or may not be the kind of people whom you would have chosen for yourself. But you have to think about your friend, who is not you and never will be you. If your friend makes new acquaintances, try not to feel jealous or threatened. Be as supportive as possible and understand that your own friendship still exists.

It's even more valuable than the new friendships your friend is making. Just be supportive, give your friend the space he or she needs, and let your friend live his or her life.

Take a good look at yourself and the new friends you have made. Remember that these friends are not a threat to your old friendships. Just look at your friends' new relationships in the same way. You are building a larger circle of friends, and that doesn't mean old friends have to be squeezed out to make room for new ones. Remember the old adage: the more the merrier.

Making Time for Each Other

One way to support a friend and strengthen a friendship is to make time for each other. Your new lives may leave you with much less time to hang out than you had in elementary school. You now have more homework, more activities that can fill your after-school hours, and weekends filled with sports, lessons, or other time commitments. Once in a while, you should take time out from these activities to simply slow down and hang out with some old pals for a while.

As with any relationship, you have to put some time and care into friendships. While you may "see" your buddies all the time on Facebook, you really need to get together to feel the one-on-one support of friendships. Laughing, hanging out, and playing video games for an afternoon might be just what your old friendships need to stay fresh and vital. And remember what is important to your friends. Making sure you don't miss their birthday parties and other special events will show your friends that you truly care about them and are fully committed to the friendship, no matter how busy you are these days.

Face time with friends is important. Hanging out and talking face-to-face is the best way to catch up and foster a good friendship.

Forgive and Forget

Even if you try to be as supportive as possible, friends are bound to have problems with each other once in a while. You may get into a fight with your friend despite all your best efforts. But don't worry. It's never too late to patch things up and forgive and forget.

Middle school friends often find themselves in jealous arguments about other friends or crushes or in conflict over how they want to spend their time. Suppose a friend does not support your desire to try out for the basketball team. He thinks you should join him in trying out for the wrestling team so that you can be together at practices and matches. You get into an argument, and you stop talking to each other. Now's the time to think about how much your friendship means to you and if the argument merits straining or even jeopardizing the relationship.

True friends learn to compromise with each other, so it is important to talk out your disagreement. Try to remain calm, even if you feel like yelling and screaming. Give the same advice to your friend. Then explain your viewpoint, and allow your friend to provide his perspective. Explain that although you would like to be with him at the wrestling meets and practices, you would be unhappy and feel like you were missing something by not pursuing what you are most interested in—basketball. Explain that there is not even any guarantee that you would make it onto the wrestling team anyway. Your friend should be able to understand your point of view.

But don't forget to ask for and seriously and compassionately consider your friend's point of view also. He may be concerned

Friends argue over many topics, including one or the other's new relationship with a member of the opposite sex. Trying to understand a friend's point of view is an important part of getting over an argument.

that you will be meeting new friends and not want to hang out with him anymore. He may feel uncomfortable going out for the wrestling team by himself. There may be important reasons why your friend was giving you a hard time about following your own dream. All you have to do is try to talk it out together. Simply trying to make him feel better could be enough to demonstrate to him that you understand and care about his feelings.

Once you and your friends have talked about your problems and worked through them, try not to dwell on them and keep

STAND UP TO BULLIES

One of the most important ways to be a good friend is to help your friends through situations in which they are being bullied or mistreated by others. It is not enough to turn away and pretend that you don't notice the problem. If you see someone being abused or mistreated in any way—even if that person is just an acquaintance or even a stranger—be a good friend. Don't look the other way. Instead, talk to your friend or acquaintance about it and explain that he or she should get help from a teacher or other adult. Bullies should not be tolerated, so you must help your friend stand up to the problem. You would appreciate it if a friend helped you to stand up to and stop a bully, so do your best to be the kind of good friend you would want in a time of need.

bringing them up. Moving on and forgetting your argument is the best way to continue to develop a strong and lasting friendship.

Friendship vs. Cliqueship

You've seen the way cliques operate. These groups of kids are led by one or two people who tell the others what to do. The members of the clique do not act like true friends to each other. You can often tell the difference between a true friendship and mere "cliqueships."

Clique members would not be supportive of something new that a member wants to take part in that lies outside the normal

Real friends treat each other like loving and supportive family members rather than as members of a club who can be kicked out for any perceived violation of the group's rules.

interests of the clique. For example, if a clique member suddenly demonstrates "nerdy" or "uncool" behavior or is friendly with someone who does, he or she is at risk of being reprimanded or rejected by the group or may even be kicked out altogether.

A true friend would not treat someone like this. A true friend would treat someone more like a family member. In a healthy and supportive family, membership is permanent, regardless of how divergent one's interests are or how unique one's attitudes and behavior. Each member of the family plays an important role, and each viewpoint is respected and valued. All members of the family work together to make the relationship work.

Academics are an important part of middle school. Helping friends study, encouraging them to complete homework, and working together to improve their grades all show that you are a good and caring friend.

Making the Grade

It is every student's responsibility to adjust to the academics of middle school, but who couldn't use a little help once in a while? Think about how uncomfortable and nerve-wracking it is to do poorly in school. You know what the sweaty palms before a test feel like, and you are probably well acquainted with the butterflies in your stomach while waiting for your test results. Or maybe you fear report card day or that upcoming oral report. If you are familiar with any of these situations, then all you have to do is remember that your friends probably feel the same way.

Talk to each other about your academic worries and fears, and help each other study.

After all, this may be the first time you are learning a foreign language or a musical instrument or giving oral presentations in front of the class. The academic workload becomes heavier in middle school, so friends may need some extra support from those who are going through it with them. Just remember that if you are providing support to your friends, you are most likely getting support in return. However, if you are giving your friends support but not receiving support from them in return, stop and think things over. You may be wasting time with the wrong friends.

10 GreAT QUESTIONS
TO ASK A MIDDLE SCHOOL GUIDANCE COUNSELOR

1 Will I ever get used to being in middle school?

2 How can I stay away from people whom I don't like?

3 How can I get other kids to like me?

4 Will I lose my old friends when I go to middle school?

5 How can I make sure that older kids don't bother me on the bus or in the hallways?

6 What should I do if I am bullied or my friends are bullied?

7 What can I do if my new friends don't get along with my old friends?

8 What if I don't get along with other kids in my class?

9 Is it important to look or act like the other kids in my school?

10 Why are some kids so mean?

CHAPTER FOUR

DEALING WITH FALSE FRIENDS

Just think of all of the good friends you can make in middle school. But how can you recognize a good friend when you see one if you don't know what a bad friend can be like? The bad friends are ones that you have to make a special effort to keep away from—for your own good! They are the cheaters, the bullies, the ones who spread rumors, and those who generally treat people like dirt.

The biggest problem of all is that you can't always immediately spot these qualities and tendencies in people. People don't wear tags that say "good guy" or "bad guy." You have to learn to recognize the more subtle signs that someone is not worth your time. But unfortunately that could take a little time, and your relationship can suffer some damage in the meantime.

Underminers

You may already be months into what you think is a great relationship with a new friend when you begin to notice that she is not who you originally thought. You may notice your friend being

You may have false friends around you. A false friend does not care about your feelings and may be manipulative or cruel.

manipulative and trying to get you to do what she wants. She may put down your other friends or tell you that she doesn't like the way you look or dress. She may try to change you or discourage you from doing the things that you are interested in. These are all signs of a defective or even toxic friendship.

You may even be inclined to think that your friend is right. Some people who are being manipulated by friends don't recognize it for a while. They may even have low self-esteem and think that their friend is justified in her criticisms or only trying to help. While it's true that good friends do try to help each other and offer helpful advice, be sure that you are aware of when your friend's comments are hurting your feelings. Your friend may not be aware of it, so let her know how her comments make you feel and give her a fair chance to be more thoughtful and kind.

WHAT A GOOD FRIEND DOES

- Listens to you
- Understands your problems
- Does not spread gossip about you
- Understands your feelings
- Forgives you when you mess up

WHAT A *NOT SO GOOD* FRIEND DOES

- Makes you feel bad about yourself
- Tells stories about you to others
- Lies to you
- Doesn't support you when you have problems
- Tells you that you should change who you are

If you do not see an improvement in your friend's behavior after you talk things through, make sure you do something about your problem. Think seriously of moving on and leaving your friendship behind. Peer pressure and negativity can make for a very difficult and awkward relationship. Very often, tweens and teens think that they are responsible for making their friends angry, when it is actually the friend who is being negative, mean-spirited, or just plain hurtful. Don't take the blame for something that is not your fault and is being done to hurt you!

Gossips and Rumor Mongers

Suppose you find out that one of your good friends is actually spreading rumors about you. He is ruining your reputation, and you are shocked to find out that he is the source of the vicious gossip. First of all, do some detective work before you accuse your friend of something serious. While it's true that behavior like this is never OK, you may be introducing some bad blood into the relationship if you mistakenly accuse your friend of something he simply didn't do. Find out where the rumor got started and how it spread. Sometimes rumors get started when information gets skewed or someone decides to bend the truth that they were told.

Once you have firmly established that your friend is the source of the rumor, it is time to take action. You need to have a conversation with your friend, but you also need to keep it as civil as possible. Try not to yell or scream at each other because it won't do much good for either of you, and it won't solve your problem at all. Instead, ask your friend why he spread the rumors about you and tell him that it hurt your feelings. Take it from there and see what happens.

If you are not feeling respected by a friend, let that friend know. Open and honest communication can help many friendships get past rough patches and grow stronger.

Sometimes people promise never to do something again to hurt you, but then you nevertheless keep getting victimized by the same person over and over again. If that is beginning to happen to you, end the friendship. Tell your friend that, though he doesn't respect you, you respect yourself. And out of self-respect, you are choosing to end the friendship. This may be difficult. He may be a friend you have had for many years. You may not have that many others to take his place. But staying in a relationship that is hurtful and unbalanced is a prescription for disaster.

Dumping the Bad Guys

So how do you end it with the bad guys? First of all, be sure that you have correctly and justifiably identified the person as someone with whom you no longer wish to associate because of negative and mean-spirited attitudes or behavior (and not because he or she isn't cool or popular enough). Once you know that you are serious about staying away from this person, you will have to make your move.

Sometimes just engaging in the argument that results from you confronting the friend can be an easy way for you to put some distance between you. Very often, people have to make a concerted effort to patch things up after an argument. If you truly don't want to patch things up, then don't respond to your friend's efforts to apologize or make things better. You might even want to tell your friend that you have had enough of this treatment and behavior and you think that you shouldn't be friends anymore.

But what happens when the person keeps calling or texting you or trying to be your friend again? Make it clear again that you don't think you were treated right and that you want him or her to stop contacting you. Try to have a heart, though. If your friend does not seem to be taking your "separation" well, be a little lenient. Talk about the problem again and think about giving him or her a second chance. It is not easy to decide when someone should get another chance, but you should know it in your heart. You will likely get a gut feeling about what you should do. Listen to your gut feeling, which may otherwise be known as "following your heart." Even if you are convinced that you can no longer be friends, end things in as sensitive, compassionate, gentle, and discreet a manner as possible.

Being Dumped by a Friend

Sure, it's not always easy to dump a friend, but think about how difficult it can be if you are the one being dumped. One-on-one, you can always talk to a friend and try to work things out. But often, a whole group of students will try to oust someone from their clique, or group. They might ignore the person or try to embarrass him or her in front of other people. Spreading rumors

Sometimes friendships do not work out. Cliques sometimes "dump" members, but some close relationships may also end. Both parties may be hurt when this happens.

or telling lies about the person are also common ways that cliques decide to dump one of their members.

If you find yourself in one of these bullying situations, be sure to tell someone about it. You should not have to suffer in silence, and you should not have to be alone in the situation. You may find that many people support you and look down on the people who are doing this to you. These true friends and sup-porters can "have your back" and give you the upper hand. They can give you just enough confidence to get through the ordeal. This united front may even get your ex-friends to stop their nasty behavior. Best of all, finding new friends is also the best way to get over losing onetime friends.

accusation A claim that someone has done something wrong.

acquaintance A person who is known but is not a close friend.

anxiety A feeling of worry.

bully A person who treats others poorly to make himself or herself feel superior. Bullying can involve verbal and/or physical intimidation and attacks.

clique A small group of people with similar interests who do not readily allow others to join them.

confrontation An argument between people or groups.

elementary school Preliminary education that stretches from kindergarten through fourth or fifth grade.

extracurricular activities The academic and athletic pursuits students engage in outside of school hours.

Facebook A social networking Web site in which people communicate with each other online. This communication includes posts, messaging, and shared photos and videos.

friend A person who knows you well; likes you; supports, encourages, and protects you; and looks out for your best interests.

gang An organized group of people who are often involved in crimes or other violent or illegal activities.

hazing The practice of forcing new or potential members of a group to do humiliating, dangerous, or violent tasks to prove that they belong.

manipulate To control or influence something or someone to achieve a desired outcome.

middle school Education that bridges elementary school and high school, usually stretching from fifth or sixth grade through eighth grade.

peer pressure Influence exerted by classmates and other people of your age to think, act, dress, or behave in a certain way, often in a manner that is in opposition to your own desires, interests, or values.

peers A group of people who about the same age and share roughly the same ability and achievement level.

self-esteem The way we view or value ourselves.

social networking The use of specially designed Web sites to keep in touch with or meet other people.

status update The latest information someone posts about himself or herself on a social networking site such as Facebook.

Twitter A social networking Web site in which people communicate their thoughts, in snippets of 140 characters or less, to others who "follow," or read and respond to, them.

unfriend To remove a friend from a list of contacts on Facebook.

Big Brothers Big Sisters of America
National Office
230 North 13th Street
Philadelphia, PA 19107
(215) 567-7000
Web site: http://www.bbbs.org
Big Brothers Big Sisters of America is a mentoring organization
in which volunteers provide advice and support to youth.

Boys & Girls Club
National Headquarters
1275 Peachtree Street NE
Atlanta, GA 30309-3506
(404) 487-5700
Web site: http://www.bgca.org
The Boys & Girls Club provides a safe venue for children to
grow and learn, as well as a way to foster ongoing relationships with caring adult professionals. The organization
offers programs and experiences designed to build character
and enhance children's lives.

Bully Beware Productions
6 Bedingfield Street
Port Moody, BC V3H 3N1
Canada
(888) 552-8559
Web site: http://www.bullybeware.com

This organization founded by British Columbia teachers produces materials and workshops about bullying prevention.

Bullying Canada
471 Smythe Street
P.O. Box 27009
Fredericton, NB E3B 9M1
Canada
(877) 352-4497
Web site: http://www.bullyingcanada.ca
Bullying Canada provides support to bullied youth through online group or one-on-one chats, newsletters, resources, stories, a phone hotline, and a video library.

Gay, Lesbian, & Straight Education Network (GLSEN)
National Headquarters
90 Broad Street, 2nd Floor
New York, NY 10004
(212) 727-0135
Web site: http://www.glsen.org
This national organization is focused on making schools safe for students of all sexual orientations and gender identities and expressions.

National Youth Leadership Council (NYLC)
1667 Snelling Avenue North
St. Paul, MN 55108

(651) 631-3672

Web site: http://www.nylc.org

The NYLC is devoted to helping young people become leaders in their communities via community involvement.

Students Against Destructive Decisions (SADD)

P.O. Box 800

Marlboro, MA 01752

(877) SADD-INC (723-3462)

Web site: http://www.saddonline.com

SADD is a student-based organization that was originally founded to combat underage drinking and drunk driving. Since then, it has expanded its mission to address issues such as drug abuse, violence, STDs, and suicide.

The Trevor Project

8704 Santa Monica Boulevard, Suite 200

West Hollywood, CA 90069

(310) 271-8846 (main office)

866-4-U-Trevor (hotline)

Web site: http://www.thetrevorproject.org

This organization runs the Trevor Lifeline, a crisis and suicide prevention hotline for youth who are gay or questioning their sexual orientation.

YMCA

5 West 63rd Street, 2nd Floor

New York, NY 10023

(212) 727-8800
(888) 477-9622
Web site: http://www.ymca.net
The YMCA offers young people a place to come after school for
 safe, productive activities that support academic achievement,
 encourage self-confidence, and develop healthy lifestyles.

Web Sites

Due to the changing nature of Internet links, Rosen Publishing
has developed an online list of Web sites related to the subject
of this book. This site is updated regularly. Please use this link
to access this list:

http://www.rosenlinks.com/MSSH/Peer

for further reading

Borgenicht, David, Ben H. Winters, and Robin Epstein. *The Worst-Case Scenario Survival Handbook: Middle School.* San Francisco, CA: Chronicle Books, 2009.

Boyett, Jason. *A Guy's Guide to Life: How to Become a Man in 224 Pages or Less.* Nashville, TN: Thomas Nelson, 2010.

Canfield, Jack, and Mark Victor Hansen. *Chicken Soup for the Soul: Teens Talk Relationships: Stories About Family, Friends, and Love.* Cos Cob, CT: Chicken Soup for the Soul Publishing, 2008.

Eastham, Chad. *The Truth About Dating, Love, and Just Being Friends.* Nashville, TN: Thomas Nelson, 2011.

Eastham, Chad, Bill Farrel, and Pam Farrel. *Guys Are Waffles, Girls Are Spaghetti.* Nashville, TN: Thomas Nelson, 2009.

Feldhahn, Jeff, Eric Rice, and Shaunti Feldhahn. *For Young Men Only: A Guy's Guide to the Alien Gender.* Colorado Springs, CO: Multnomah Books, 2008.

Fox, Annie. *Be Confident in Who You Are* (Middle School Confidential). Minneapolis, MN: Free Spirit Publishing, 2008.

Fox, Annie. *Real Friends vs. the Other Kind* (Middle School Confidential). Minneapolis, MN: Free Spirit Publishing, 2009.

Fox, Annie. *What's Up with My Family?* (Middle School Confidential). Minneapolis, MN: Free Spirit Publishing, 2010.

Heiden, Pete. *I Luv U 2: Understanding Relationships and Dating* (Essential Health: A Guy's Guide). Edina, MN: ABDO Publishing, 2010.

Jacobs, Thomas A. *Teen Cyberbullying Investigated: Where Do Your Rights End and Consequences Begin?* Minneapolis, MN: Free Spirit Publishing, 2010.

Ludwig, Trudy. *Confessions of a Former Bully.* New York, NY: Tricycle Press, 2010.

Miller, Karren. *Male and Female Roles* (Opposing Viewpoints). Farmington Hills, MI: Greenhaven, 2009.

Mosatache, Harriet S., and Karen Unger. *Too Old for This, Too Young for That!: Your Survival Guide for the Middle School Years.* Minneapolis, MN: Free Spirit Publishing, 2010.

Patterson, James. *Middle School: The Worst Years of My Life.* New York, NY: Little, Brown & Company, 2011.

Rivero, Lisa. *Smart Teens' Guide to Living with Intensity: How to Get More Out of Life and Learning.* Scottsdale, AZ: Great Potential Press, 2010.

Simmons, Danette. *Teen Reflections: My Life, My Journey, My Story.* Charleston, SC: CreateSpace, 2010.

Tompkins, Michael A., and Katherine A. Martinez. *My Anxious Mind: A Teen's Guide to Managing Anxiety and Panic.* Washington, DC: Magination Press, 2009.

Williams, Julie. *A Smart Girl's Guide to Starting Middle School: Everything You Need to Know About Juggling More Homework, More Teachers, and More Friends!* Middleton, WI: American Girl, 2004.

bibliography

Bruzzese, Joe. *Parents' Guide to the Middle School Years.* Berkeley, CA: Celestial Arts, 2009.

BusyMommyMedia.com. "How to Help Your Tween Build Healthy Friendships." September 24, 2008. Retrieved February 2012 (http://busymommymedia.com/2009/09/how-to-help-your-tween-build-healthy-friendships).

Erlbach, Arlene. *The Middle School Survival Guide.* New York, NY: Walker and Company, 2003.

Espeland, Pamela. *Making Choices and Making Friends: The Social Competencies Assets.* Minneapolis, MN: Free Spirit Publishing, 2006.

Farell, Juliana, et al. *Middle School: The Real Deal: From Cafeteria Food to Combination Locks.* New York, NY: Collins, 2007.

Fox, Annie, and Ruth Kirschner. *Too Stressed to Think? A Teen Guide to Staying Sane When Life Makes You Crazy.* Minneapolis, MN: Free Spirit Publishing, 2005.

Gephart, Donna. *How to Survive Middle School.* New York, NY: Yearling, 2011.

Kaufman, Gershen. *Stick Up for Yourself: Every Kid's Guide to Personal Power & Positive Self-Esteem.* Minneapolis, MN: Free Spirit Publishing, 1999.

Kelly, Marguerite. "Trouble Adjusting to Middle School." *Bangor Daily News*, February 20, 2012. Retrieved February 2012 (http://bangordailynews.com/2012/02/20/health/trouble-adjusting-to-middle-school).

KidsHealth.org. "Coping with Cliques." Retrieved February 2012 (http://kidshealth.org/teen/your_mind/problems/cliques.html).

Kilpatrick, Haley, and Whitney Joiner. *The Drama Years: Real Girls Talk About Surviving Middle School—Bullies, Brands, Body Image, and More*. New York, NY: Free Press, 2012.

Scholastic. "Making the Transition: Help Your Child Navigate These Typical Middle-School Challenges." Retrieved February 2012 (http://www.scholastic.com/resources/article /making-the-transition).

TweenParent.com. "Helping Your Preteen Cope with Feeling Left Out." Retrieved February 2012 (http://www .tweenparent.com/articles/view/34).

U.S. News & World Report. "6 Ways Parents Can Help Kids Cope with Social Cruelty." February 5, 2010. Retrieved February 2012 (http://health.usnews.com/health -news/blogs/on-parenting/2010/02/05/6-ways-parents -can-help-kids-cope-with-social-cruelty).

index

About the Authors

Kathy and Adam Furgang are a married couple who wish they met each other in middle school. They both write teen-oriented educational books on topics such as nutrition, economics, family relationships, the environment, and careers. They live in upstate New York with their two sons, one of whom is adjusting smoothly to life in middle school.

Photo Credits

Cover © iStockphoto.com/digitalskillet; pp. 3, 4–5 © iStockphoto.com/Jose Gil; p. 8 Laurence Mouton/PhotoAlto Agency RF Collections/Getty Images; p. 10 KidStock/Blend Images/Getty Images; p. 13 © iStockphoto.com/kristian sekulic; p. 14 © iStockphoto.com/Catherine Yeulet; pp. 16–17 Brendan O'Sullivan/Photolibrary/Getty Images;p. 21 BananaStock/Thinkstock; p. 23 Jutta Klee/Taxi/Getty Images; pp. 24–25 Yellow Dog Productions/The Image Bank/Getty Images; pp. 28–29 Digital Vision/Thinkstock; p. 33 Comstock/Thinkstock; p. 36 Jupiterimages/Photos.com/Thinkstock; p. 38 Toby Burrows/Photodisc/Thinkstock; p. 40 iStockphoto/Thinkstock; p. 41 Jupiterimages/liquidlibrary/Thinkstock; p. 45 Wavebreak Media/Thinkstock; p. 48 SW Productions/Photodisc/Getty Images; p. 50 © David Young-Wolff/PhotoEdit; cover and interior graphics (arrows) © iStockphoto.com/alekup.

Designer: Nicole Russo; Photo Researcher: Marty Levick